The Hit and Run GANG 1
NEW KID IN TOWN

Don't Miss Any of the
On-the-Field Excitement with
THE HIT AND RUN GANG
by Steven Kroll
from Avon Books
(#2) PLAYING FAVORITES
(#3) THE SLUMP
(#4) THE STREAK

STEVEN KROLL grew up in New York City, where he was a pretty good first baseman and #3 hitter on baseball teams in Riverside Park. He graduated from Harvard University, spent almost seven years as an editor in book publishing, and then became a full-time writer. He is the author of more than fifty books for young people. He and his wife Abigail live in New York City and root for the Mets.

The Hit and Run GANG ① NEW KID IN TOWN

STEVEN KROLL

Illustrated by Meredith Johnson

AN AVON CAMELOT BOOK

For Abigail

THE HIT AND RUN GANG #1: NEW KID IN TOWN is an original publication of
Avon Books. This work has never before appeared in book form.

AVON BOOKS
A division of
The Hearst Corporation
1350 Avenue of the Americas
New York, New York 10019

Contents

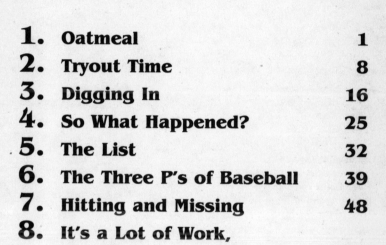

CONTENTS

1. Oatmeal

Phil Hubbard rolled out of bed and pulled on his clothes: sweatshirt, jeans, sneakers. It was a chilly Saturday morning in early April, tryout day for the Rah Rah Rockets of the Tri-City Junior League.

Phil had been waiting for this moment for weeks. He'd only just moved to Raymond-town a month ago, but almost the first thing he'd heard was—oh, those Rah Rah Rockets! They were really the Raymondtown Rock-ets, of course. Everyone just liked the way they played so much, they had to have a nickname.

Baseball was Phil's great love. He watched the major league games on TV. Sometimes he wore his glove around the house just for the feel of it and the smell of the leather. His old hometown had been too small to have a team for kids. All he could do was play catch and hit fly balls in the park with his friend Danny. Now he had the chance to make a team!

Phil really wanted that. Things hadn't been going so well since he came to Raymondtown. To start with, he hadn't even wanted to come. But one night his dad, who sold computers for a big company, came home and said, "They want me to take over a new department. We'll be moving next month."

Phil was so shocked he didn't know what to say. All he knew was he'd have to leave school in the middle of the year and he'd lose all his friends. He'd have to go to some new town and some new school and there would be strange people and everything would be scary and weird.

And that was what happened. Phil and his parents moved, and everything in their old life disappeared. Their new house was so new, it smelled funny. The new

2

neighborhood was pretty, with lots of nice big trees, but Phil and his parents didn't know anyone there. Phil's new school looked just like his old school, with long hallways and classrooms on either side. But even after his new teacher, Mrs. Irvington, introduced him to the class, he just took a seat in the back and didn't speak to anyone.

He was little and shy. He was doing okay in his third grade schoolwork, but he still didn't have any friends.

"Philip! Breakfast!"

"Coming, Mom!"

Phil finished tying his sneakers and dashed over to the closet. He pulled on his old baseball glove and pounded the pocket a few times. But where was his favorite bat?

He rummaged around in the closet, pushing away clothes, shoes, a half-deflated basketball. A sweater fell on his head. No bat. Where could it be? How could he go to tryouts without it? He'd have to use one of the

bats that were there. Suppose there wasn't one the right size?

"Philip!"

He hurried into the bathroom, balanced his glove on the edge of the bathtub, washed his face, brushed his teeth, and ran down the stairs to have breakfast with his parents.

They were both at the table when he got there. His dad was eating a piece of toast and looking at the newspaper. His mom was taking a sip of coffee. When she saw him, she got up and began bustling around the stove.

"I've made you some oatmeal," she said. "It'll warm you up and stick to your ribs."

"Oh, Mom. You know I don't like oatmeal."

"That's not true. You liked it the last time, especially when I put the spoon of honey on top."

"But it's so gluey."

She came over and hugged him. "That's what makes it stick, silly. If you're going to make that team, you have to have a good breakfast. Now sit down, drink your juice, and I'll have this ready in a minute."

Phil sat and took a sip of orange juice.

"Morning, son," said his dad. "What position are you trying out for today?"

"Infield, I guess. Maybe third base."

Phil stuck his glove under his chair. His dad wiped his rimless glasses and ran his fingers through his short blond hair. "I was a pretty good second baseman myself once. Wish I could get in some playing time with you now."

Phil's face lit up. "That would be great."

"Well, maybe one day soon."

There was the oatmeal. There was the spoon. Phil put in some honey and some milk. Then he glanced at the kitchen clock.

Nine already! He wolfed down the oatmeal. As he reached for his glass of milk, he spilled it.

"Philip," said his mom, "try to relax. Try to have fun. Promise me."

"I have to go," Phil said. "I have to make the team."

He reached for his glove and grabbed his cap as he ran for the door. When he got outside, he stepped back and opened the door again.

"Thanks for breakfast!" he shouted. Then he was off on his bike for the ballfield.

2. Tryout Time

The Junior League ballfield was downtown behind the IGA store. It was only about five blocks from Phil's house, but he pedaled hard all the way. He didn't want to risk being later than he already was. He didn't want to look bad before he'd even begun.

When he arrived, a lot of kids were already out practicing. A coach was hitting fly balls to a bunch of hopeful outfielders. There was a kid at every infield position, and another coach was standing at home plate hitting ground balls to them.

Phil noticed there was a girl at second base. She was little and cute and had short dark hair sticking out from under her baseball cap. A sharply hit ground ball came right at her. She gobbled it up and fired the ball to first. Another shot bounced wide to her left. She dove for it and pegged a bullet to first from her knees.

"Atta way, Vicky!" someone shouted from the sidelines. "Atta way to play!"

Phil wished he could be that good, wished people would shout his name when he fired to first for the out. Just then he didn't know what to do. Should he join the bunch of kids shagging flies in the outfield? Should he wait for a turn in the infield?

He did a few warm-up stretches, some jumping jacks and push-ups. Then he watched the three pitchers warming up on the sidelines.

One was a tall, muscular kid with a shock of black hair he kept wiping out of his eyes. Phil remembered him from school. His name was Andy McClellan, and boy, could he throw smoke. He had a big motion, he brought the ball right over the top, and the sound of it smacking the catcher's mitt could practically be heard across the street.

After one hard fastball, the catcher had to take his hand out of the mitt and shake it around.

Then there were two kids Phil didn't know. The first was big and blond. His delivery was slow and steady, and even though he didn't throw hard, he seemed to throw nothing but strikes. The other was short, dark, and stubby, with a long, narrow face and a crazy sidearm delivery. He looked as if he'd be really wild, but most of his pitches seemed to end up near the strike zone.

Phil was still watching when a car door slammed and an arm came around his shoulders.

"Hey, what's happenin'?"

He turned as an ancient blue Buick bounced out of the parking lot. There was a short black kid, built like a fireplug, he'd seen at school.

"I'm Lucas Emory, but everyone calls me Luke. You're the new kid, aren't you? I've seen you at school. So you like to play baseball. Well, I'll tell you one thing. Coach Channing—he's the manager of the team—is a very fair man."

They shook hands.

Phil blinked. He'd only just opened his mouth to speak when a tall, thin man with a black beard blew a whistle from the pitcher's mound.

"Okay," he said, "time we got this show on the road. Everyone will sign the tryout sheet"—he held up a clipboard with a sheet of paper attached—"and everyone will have a shot at every position. If they wish, the kids in their present positions will start in them. Everyone will hit—hit three and bunt three—and run out your last swing. Fifteen of you will be chosen for the team. My assistant coaches are Jack Carr and Herman Lopez"—they both stepped forward and tipped their caps—"and I'm the head coach and manager, Ron Channing."

At first no one moved, as if it still wasn't clear what to do. Then, suddenly, everyone was lining up to sign the tryout sheet.

Phil stood behind Luke, who was talking to the kid in front of him now, but they were pretty far back. When he finally reached Coach Channing and signed the sheet, the coach smiled down at him.

"So you want to make this team?"

"Yes, sir," Phil replied.

"Well, I wish you luck."

"Thanks."

It felt like a good omen. Coach Channing wasn't saying that to everyone. A moment later, the infield was filled with kids again. Three other kids turned up in the outfield and one of them was Luke, pounding his glove and shouting for the ball to be hit to him. None of this mattered to Phil. As he walked off the field and waited for his turn, he hoped the good omen would see him through.

He had to wait for some time. Coach Lopez was down the left field sideline, working with the pitchers in the makeshift bull pen. Kids who weren't in the field could go stand at the plate so the pitcher could throw to a batter, but Phil wasn't keen on that. He wanted to see how the other kids did in the field.

As Coach Carr stood at home plate fungoing the ball, he watched that girl Vicky turn a few more great plays at second base. Then he watched Luke make a long running catch of a fly ball to left center. After that, he started watching the chunky kid with glasses and a dirty face who was playing short.

The kid was everywhere at once, smothering the ball and firing to first. An infield pop-up, and he was under it for the out. A grounder to his left, and he was there. Then Coach Carr hit a sharp ground ball between short and third. The kid went deep in the hole to his right, backhanded the ball, and threw. It was a perfect throw, but the first baseman dropped the ball. Even so, everyone cheered.

Wow, Phil thought. This is going to be a tough infield to make, but at least the guy on third keeps bobbling the ball. Third, of course, was what he really wanted.

A big, heavyset kid was standing next to him. Phil looked up. "Do you know who's at short?" he asked, "And who's the girl at second?"

The big kid's face turned into a snarl. "What's it to you, shrimp?"

Phil was stunned. "I just wanted to know."

"Brian Krause and Vicky Lopez."

The big head turned away. It didn't turn back.

Phil wondered what was eating this guy, but it didn't surprise him that Vicky was probably the coach's daughter.

The fielders rotated and rotated again as outfielders replaced infielders and infielders left for the sidelines. Finally, ever so finally, Phil heard, "Hubbard, Phil Hubbard, right field, please."

Phil took a deep breath. "All right," he said to himself, "here we go."

3. Digging In

Right field was a million miles from home plate. He didn't want to be an outfielder. What was he doing way out here?

Coach Carr hit an easy fly ball right at him. He reached up and caught it one-handed, pegged the ball to second. So far, so good.

He played a little shallower, and the coach hit a fly over his head. He went back, back, got under it, reached up his glove, and the ball skittered off the heel!

Phil was so upset, he threw wildly and the ball caromed off the backstop. He figured he'd better play deeper and the coach poked a little looper just over the first base-man's head.

Phil came charging in. "I've got it!" he

shouted, calling the first baseman off. He dove, but the ball was beyond his reach. It bounced off his glove and rolled into the outfield grass. Two flubs in a row.

He caught a few more fly balls as he was rotated around the outfield. He made a sharp play on a ground ball hit up the middle when he was in center, getting down on one knee and hitting the cut-off man at second base. Nothing quite made up for those errors.

Now he was at third. Where he wanted to be. Here was his chance!

Coach Carr hit a slow roller down the line. Phil charged it, barehanded it, and threw!

The throw was wide of the bag at first. The ball landed in the bleachers.

Oh, no. Not now.

Another ground ball, this time to his left. He moved over, kept the ball in front of him, made the perfect throw.

That's it. That's the way, but now another ground ball was coming and it was coming right at him! He was playing deep, on the edge of the outfield grass, but the ball was hit hard, a real screamer, and as he went for it, it took a bad hop. Quickly, defensively, he turned his head away. The ball scooted by him into left field.

Phil's shoulders slumped. He looked at the ground, not wanting to have to look at the others and read their faces. But here was the left fielder heaving the ball back to the infield. Phil caught the ball smartly with one hand and rifled it to the catcher.

At least that was better, and so was the line drive he caught that was nearly over his head, and the neat double play ball he fielded and tossed to the second baseman while he was playing short, and the scoop of a ball out of the dirt that he made when he moved over to first. He knew he was too small to play first, and right-handed besides, but the play made him feel more confident.

Not a whole lot, though. When he walked off the field, there was Luke.

"Hey, how's it goin'?"

Phil shook his head. "Not so good."

"Yeah, I noticed, but you looked pretty good most of the time. Wait till you dazzle everyone with your hitting."

For some reason this made Phil feel even worse. When, a few minutes later, Coach Channing announced it was time to hit, he took his place in line with more than a few butterflies in his stomach.

The kids in the field would stay in the field until it was their turn to hit. Coach Channing would tell them when to come in, and he would send out replacements. The coaches would do most of the pitching. The pitchers trying out would do the rest. Now who was going to catch?

"I'll catch."

It was Luke, of course. As he put on the gear, squatted down behind the plate, and made a target for the ball with his mitt, he looked as if he'd been born to the job.

Phil was batting behind the big, fat kid who had been so mean to him before. Sure enough, his personality didn't improve at the plate. He smacked Coach Lopez's first pitch deep into left field, but when he took a huge cut and missed the next one, he swore. Then he belted a line drive over the second baseman's head, missed two bunts in a row, and stormed out of the batter's box.

With that, Coach Channing grabbed him by the shoulder and gave him a warning. He got back in the box, bunted down the third base line, and ran meekly to first.

"That Pete Wyshansky, he's nothing but trouble," said the boy who came to take Phil's place in the on-deck circle. "Good ballplayer, though."

Phil realized the boy was Brian Krause, the dirty-faced kid he'd been watching at short.

"You're pretty good yourself."

"Thanks," said Brian. He smiled. "Good luck at the plate."

Phil was pretty sure he was going to need it. Waiting in the on-deck circle, he'd put on a batting helmet and swung with every pitch Coach Lopez threw to Wyshansky. He'd also put the doughnut on the end of his bat and taken a few swings with the extra weight, but he hadn't been able to find a twenty-six inch bat like his favorite. He'd settled for a twenty-eight he knew was too heavy. Stepping into the batter's box, he tried to think positive.

He anchored his back foot near the back line, kept his arms back and the bat almost straight up in the air. He wasn't really sure why he was using this stance. He'd seen some major leaguers use it on TV, and when he'd been up before, it seemed to make pitchers nervous. Right now, though, it just made holding the heavy bat a little easier.

He tried to concentrate. He knew that concentrating and keeping your eye on the ball were the most important parts of good hitting. Coach Lopez wound and threw. The pitch was down and away, but Phil reared back and lunged at it. The ball landed with a smack in Luke's mitt.

Up until now Phil had been concentrating

too hard to pay any attention to Luke. Now he smiled sadly back at him.

"Don't keep your bat head so high," Luke whispered. "You'll never hit a melon standing that way."

Phil brought the bat down, moved his front foot forward, and felt more comfortable standing up there. But the bat was just too heavy. The next pitch was a fastball down the middle, and he couldn't get around on it. He fouled it off down the first base line.

He dug in and smacked a change-up to short, an easy ground ball and an easy out at first. At least he'd hit something, but the next pitch was another change and he went all the way around without getting a piece of it.

He was trying not to panic. He clenched the bat in his hands and swung through another fastball. Then he popped up to second and hit a little checked-swing squibber down the first base line.

"Okay," said Coach Lopez, "now bunt,"

and the bottom dropped out. With each pitch, Phil squared around to bunt, but he couldn't seem to get the bat on the ball. He was always too high or too low. Finally he got a piece of one and foul-tipped it into Luke's mitt.

Luke tossed the ball back to the mound. Coach Lopez stepped forward. "Try very hard on this one, Phil. If you make contact, run it out."

Phil felt foolish having to be told, but he stepped in, squared around, and laid one down—a little too hard—toward third base. It bounced right to the third baseman, who had an easy play at first. Phil stopped running before he even got there.

He pulled off his batting helmet and slumped onto the bench.

"It's all over," he said to himself, trying not to cry.

4. So What Happened?

Coach Channing was standing on the mound again, and he was blowing his whistle.

"Tryouts are now over. The list of those who made the Rockets will be posted at the community center Monday morning. Thank you all for coming down. I hope you had fun, because fun and playing together are what this team is about."

"Yeah, sure, thanks a lot, I'll just go drown myself in the river," Phil said to himself as he got up off the bench, pounded the pocket of his glove, and headed for home.

He'd seen Brian Krause drive three straight pitches to the same spot in right field. He'd seen Luke weigh into the batter's box—Brian took over as catcher so he could—

and watched him crush what would have been a double into deep center. He'd seen Andy McClellan take the left fielder to the fence. He knew now, if he hadn't known before, that there was no chance, no chance at all, that he was going to make the Rah Rah Rockets.

He biked through the parking lot and out onto Market Street. He didn't want to talk to any of the guys, didn't want to rehash anything that had happened, didn't want to show his pain or try to laugh it off.

He would never laugh again. He might never talk again. He pedaled with his head down, his glove in the basket in front of him. Every so often he banged the handlebars. When he reached his house, he threw his glove against the door before he climbed the stairs.

The door opened. "What's going on?" said his mother.

"Oh, Mom," said Phil, and ran into her arms.

They went into the kitchen together. Phil

sat quietly at the table as his mother made him a tuna fish sandwich and poured a glass of milk. He knew he was thirsty and would have liked some water or a glass of Coke, but he didn't have the energy to mention that. He just sat and waited for the sandwich and the milk.

When they came, he took a swallow of milk. "I don't think I can eat the sandwich," he said. He buried his head in his hands.

His mother sat beside him. She put her arm around his shoulders. "Phil, tell me," she said.

So he told her about the errors he'd made in the field and the heavy bat and the way he just couldn't seem to get a solid hit and the embarrassment bunting.

"But Coach Channing has to choose fifteen team members. Maybe he saw your potential and you'll still make it."

"Never. It won't happen."

"Stranger things have happened."

Phil smiled. "Thanks for saying that, Mom."

He was starting to feel hungry. He ate

the tuna fish sandwich and followed it with an apple. Then he excused himself and went to take a shower.

When dinnertime rolled around, he was feeling better. Until his father, sitting across the table from him, asked, "So what happened?"

The question hung in the air.

"I played horribly," Phil said.

"Horribly?"

"Yeah. I'll never make the team."

There was a silence. Then his dad said, "You know, I didn't make the team my first time out either."

"You didn't?"

"No, but I practiced very hard and I made it the second time."

"No kidding."

Phil didn't see how he'd get a second chance. The Rockets didn't take anyone over the age of nine. Besides, how could he practice without any friends to practice with? But it helped to know that his dad understood.

At the end of dinner, Mom said, "Remember, Phil, we're going over to see Aunt Jane and Uncle Harry tomorrow afternoon."

Gloom again. Aunt Jane and Uncle Harry lived in the next town. They were funny round people, but they had a skinny weed of a son named Allen. Allen was mean and awful and a baseball buff besides. Phil knew what his first question would be.

And he was right. No sooner had the Hubbards arrived and taken off their coats than Allen said, "Did you make the Rockets?"

"Tryouts were yesterday. I don't know yet."

Allen smirked. "I bet you didn't make it. I bet you screwed up. Didn't you? I bet you did."

Right then and there Phil wanted to punch Allen in the mouth. He turned away and said nothing, but the hurt and the sadness felt worse. Allen was such a creep, and when the truth came out, he would have to know.

Aunt Jane and Uncle Harry lived in a lit-

tle house with lots of little things in it. They served a little tray of pastries and tea. Phil ate a pastry. He didn't much like tea, but he had a cup. The rest of the time he sat quietly at the table. He wanted to disappear so far into himself no one would know he was there.

Going home in the car, he felt very warm. As his father turned into their driveway, he realized that tomorrow he would have to go to school. He would see Luke and Brian and . . .

"Mom," he said when they were inside, "I'm not feeling well. Maybe I'll stay home tomorrow."

5. The List

Mom said, "Phil, I think we'd better talk about this in your room."

They walked back there together and sat on the bed. "You went out and did your best, right?" she said.

"Yes."

"Anyone who does his best has nothing to be ashamed of, right?"

"Yes."

"Everyone you know will respect you for having done your best."

"Yes," said Phil, but he thought of Allen and Pete Wyshansky and wasn't so sure.

"So you'll go tomorrow?"

Phil nodded.

"Good. I'm proud of you."

She hugged him as she left the room, but

when she dropped him off at school the next morning, she didn't know he was a bundle of nerves. Who would be the first kid he met? What would they say to each other?

He walked inside.

"Hey, what's happenin'?"

He should have known it would be Luke, who went on as usual without stopping. "I missed you after the tryouts. A few of the guys came back to my house. I wanted you to be there."

"You did?"

"Oh, come on. You weren't that bad."

Well, that sounded okay, but when they reached Mrs. Irvington's room, someone gave a loud raspberry. He turned, and Pete Wyshansky said, "Hey, look, it's the bunt-less wonder!"

Every head shot up. Every eye was on him, even the eyes of kids who wouldn't know what a bunt was. Phil's face went very red. He slunk into his seat.

For the rest of the morning, everything

was a blur. Spelling, reading, science, he might just as well have stayed home. All he could think about was Wyshansky and the bunts *he* had missed and what he might do next. So much for what Mom said about respect.

Amazingly, Pete didn't do anything next. That gave Phil more time to worry about *the list* and having to go look at it after school.

At lunch Brian and Luke sat down with him in the cafetorium. Phil was surprised that even in school, Brian's face wasn't completely free of dirt.

"We're going over to the center together," Brian said. "Want to come along?"

Didn't they know he wouldn't be on the list? Didn't they know he wouldn't want to see it with them? "Thanks," he said, "but I've got stuff to do. I'll go by later."

"You can always change your mind," Luke said. "Just let us know."

During recess he played alone on the jungle gym. In music he didn't sing. In art he drew a big question mark in the middle of the paper.

"What does that mean?" asked Mr. Pollard, the art teacher.

"Anything you want," Phil said.

Finally school let out. The community center was on Market Street near the ballfield. It was a long walk, and Phil made it even longer. He went across Pike and down Bedford and doubled back on Fitzgibbon. He also took it slow. Every kid who had tried out would be piling into the center to look at that list. He wanted to be last. He didn't want anyone else there when he was there.

No one was, and as he went up the steps, he found himself feeling more hopeful. Maybe he hadn't done as badly as he thought. He'd made a good catch out of that line drive. At least, when he hit the ground ball to short, he'd hit it hard.

He walked down the long corridor to the bulletin board. The list was up in the corner on the right. He scanned it once, very quickly. There were Luke and Brian, Pete

Wyshansky, Vicky Lopez, Andy McClellan, and the side-arm throwing Josh Rubin. He looked again and read slowly through the names. As he'd suspected all along, his name was missing.

He felt dizzy. His stomach began to churn, and he leaned his forehead against the bulletin board.

Of course he'd wanted to be wrong. He'd wanted to come in, find his name on the list, and have all his misery wiped away. Instead, he would take the long walk home.

He started back down the corridor. As he reached the front door, it opened.

"Well, hello," said Coach Channing.

Phil stared up at him with his mouth open. He swallowed hard. "Hi," he said, and ran out the door.

He ran and ran, ran as fast as he could and as far, ran until his lungs hurt and he was home. Facing Coach Channing was the final blow. He let himself into the house, went straight to his room, and threw himself on the bed.

37

He must have been lying there for half an hour with the pillow over his head when the phone rang.

His mother knocked on his door. "Philip, are you there? It's for you."

He struggled up, got himself into the kitchen, picked up the receiver. "Hello?"

"Phil? It's Luke."

"Oh, hi."

"Want to play some ball?"

Phil paused. "Didn't you see the list?"

"Sure. So what?"

"Well—"

"Look, do you want to play or not?"

"Yeah."

"Then get your butt down to the ballfield right away."

Luke hung up. Phil stood looking at the receiver. He smiled for the first time all day. Luke wanted to play ball with him, even though he wasn't a Rah Rah Rocket!

6. The Three P's of Baseball

Phil tied his sneakers tighter and pulled out his glove. "I'll be home for dinner!" he shouted as he left the house.

He jumped on his bike. He hadn't made the team, but there would still be baseball in his life. But why was Luke doing this? Was he just taking pity on a kid who couldn't hack it?

He cruised into the parking lot behind the ballfield, still pedaling at full speed and not even out of breath. He was hardly aware he'd come as far as he had. When he reached the backstop, he saw Luke standing at the plate. He wasn't alone.

Brian Krause was catching, and the big blond kid Phil had seen throw nothing but strikes was on the mound. In the field, playing shortstop, was a skinny girl with dirty blond hair in a pony tail. Phil thought he'd seen her at tryouts, but he couldn't remember for sure. As he watched, the big blond kid wound and threw, and Luke punched a ground ball to short. The girl fielded it neatly and tossed the ball back to the pitcher.

"Good going," Luke said, "but you didn't get down far enough, Jenny, didn't bend your knees. Remember, you have to play the ball. You can't let the ball play you."

He noticed Phil. "Hi. You know Brian, of course, but I don't think you've met the Carr twins."

Everyone gathered around home plate, and Luke introduced Phil to Justin and Jennifer Carr.

"So," said Luke, "ready to get started?"

"Sure," said Phil. "What are we getting started at?"

Luke laughed. "I guess I didn't tell you. Here's the deal. We all know you didn't make the team. We all think you could be good with a little help. Team practices are Tuesday, Wednesday, and Friday after school. We can meet you here on Monday, Thursday, and Saturday for two weeks until the games begin. We can work on some stuff. I'll be sort of unofficial coach. I know a lot about the game because my dad used to play semi-pro. We'll see what happens. Maybe Coach Channing will change his mind."

Phil was flattered. He was also puzzled. "Look," he said, "it's really neat you want to do this, but why are you bothering? I mean, you know Coach Channing won't change his mind. Those decisions are final."

Luke shrugged. "You're probably right about the coach, but there's always Senior League next year, and you want to be a better ballplayer, don't you?"

"We need extra practice," said Jenny Carr. "Why shouldn't we include you?"

"Mostly it's because we like you," said Brian. "We want to have fun, and we like you."

"Yeah, that's it," Luke said, smiling and putting his arm around Phil's shoulder, "we like you. Now—any more questions?"

Phil was suddenly grinning. He felt as if the sun had come out and was shining all over him, even though it was late afternoon. "No," he said, "no more questions."

"Good," said Luke. "First we have to work on your throwing. You made some lousy throws at tryouts. It looked like you had your mechanics wrong. Brian, show Phil how you hold the ball."

Brian took the ball in his right hand and held it out with his two middle fingers over the seams with a space between them.

"Okay," said Luke, "throw."

Brian gripped the ball in his glove. He had his legs apart and his weight on the balls of his feet. He pointed his left shoulder toward Justin about fifteen feet away and kept his eyes on him as he brought the ball back, bent his right knee, and shifted his weight to his back foot. Then he strode for-ward, brought his arm up and forward, released the ball with a snap of the wrist, and followed through. The throw was a perfect strike.

"You try," Luke said to Phil.

Phil took the ball. He could see the difference immediately. He hadn't been watching his target. He hadn't been shifting his weight or following through. For a few minutes he threw back and forth to Justin. Then all five kids fanned out into the infield and took turns firing the ball to first and down to Luke at home plate. Crisp, strong throws.

Phil was at third base, and after a while, Luke said, "Lookin' good, Phil. Now let's practice fielding some ground balls."

Luke hit a high bouncer to Brian at shortstop and a one-hopper to Jenny at second. Both fired bullets to Justin at first.

"See how their knees were bent and their legs were wide apart?" said Luke. "They were on the balls of their feet. When the ball came, they charged it, got down for it, kept it in front of them, made sure their gloves were down and under the ball. They looked that ball all the way into their gloves and made sure their throwing hands were on top. Then they brought the ball in and got off those throws. When you stay on top of the ball, Phil, you never turn your head away."

Phil's face burned as he remembered try-outs. He nodded to Luke, who promptly smacked one at him.

He was there. He got down. The ball was in his glove. The throw was perfect.

"Atta way," said Luke. "Good start."

They rotated around the infield, with everyone getting a chance to hit as well. Phil began to feel more comfortable with the rhythm of fielding the ball and timing his throw. They worked on different situations, too, so it wasn't all throws to first. Luke would shout "Two outs, man on second," or "One out, second and third," and whoever got the ball would have to make the right play. It even got kind of exciting as the plays came bang, bang, one after

the other and you never knew if you'd get the call.

When it was time for Phil to hit, Luke said, "Just relax and meet the ball. We'll work more on hitting on Thursday."

Phil was sure Luke was imagining him standing at the plate with the fungo bat and missing! He didn't. He did fine.

Then Luke said, "Okay, outfield practice. We'll have two outfielders, a cut-off man, and a catcher. I'll start off as the batter, and we'll rotate. Phil, you start in the outfield."

When he got out there, Luke said, "I know you know to catch balls below your waist with the fingers of your glove down and balls above your waist with the fingers of your glove up, but you've forgotten that you catch fly balls with both hands. You guide your glove with your throwing hand, and you get that hand on top of the ball as soon as it lands in your glove. Those fancy one-hand stabs make for fancy one-hand misses."

Phil nodded. The first fly ball hit out to

him, he caught cleanly and fired to Jenny, the relay man, who fired to Justin, the catcher. Of course they got their runner, trying to score from third.

They shagged fly balls for a while, getting into good position for each one. They did a pepper drill, with four fielders in a semicircle and a batter facing them. A fielder threw the ball at half speed to the batter, who hit it at half speed to another fielder, who threw it to the batter again. Good for the reflexes, Luke said, good for eye and hand coordination.

All too soon, it started to get dark. "Gotta go," Luke said. "Let's meet here Thursday after school. Like my dad says, there are the three p's of baseball: practice, practice, and practice. Phil, you look better already."

As the five of them left the field, Phil noticed an old white Chevy parked by the outfield fence.

7. Hitting and Missing

When Phil got home, he slumped into his favorite chair in the living room. He was tired. He was sweaty and dirty and sore. And he felt terrific.

"I guess you had a good time," said his mom.

Phil grinned.

"I'm glad. Looks like you found some friends, too."

Phil didn't want to push it, didn't want to admit anything. "I hope so," he said.

He couldn't wait for Thursday. He hung out with Luke and Brian at school, trading jokes as they poked one another in the ribs. He threw pop flies to himself in the backyard—and caught them. He went looking all over the house for his favorite bat and finally found it in the laundry room, where someone had put it by mistake. Once he had the bat, he practiced his swing, over and over again.

Finally it was time. He raced down to the ballfield. No one was there.

He couldn't believe it. After all that, they'd abandoned him. He looked around the empty bleachers. He trotted around the bases. It was so quiet.

He sat down on home plate, and suddenly there they were, laughing, talking, bearing down on him from the parking lot. He felt so relieved, he could have hugged them all.

"Hey, Phil, whatcha doin' on home plate?"

It was Luke, of course, always the first to speak.

"Sorry we're late. We went over to the center to pick up the catcher's gear, but the storeroom door was locked and we had to go find the secretary, Mrs. Wilson, who had the key, but she was in the ladies' room and we had to wait for her, so it took a lot of time. Anyway, we're here now. Waiting long?"

Phil let the words wash over him. "Just a few minutes," he said.

"That's good, let's start right in. We'll all get to hit, but Phil, I want you to start. Brian will pitch, Justin at first, Jenny at short, I'll catch. Later on I want Justin to pitch some, so you can try hitting a lefty."

Phil stepped into the batter's box. He anchored his back foot and got set.

"Okay," Luke said, "right away that looks better than tryouts. Your arms are back and ready. Your bat head's not up so high."

"I didn't have my bat then," Phil explained.

"I see. You could have tried choking up, but it doesn't matter. Move your front foot forward a little. Relax in there, be comfortable. When the pitcher goes into his windup, shift your weight to your back foot. Then, as he delivers, stride forward with your front foot and meet the ball with a good level swing. Turn your right shoulder into the pitch, and snap your wrists as you follow through."

Phil tried it. Then Luke got up and

showed him, holding his arms. "Okay, Brian, fire away."

Brian had been warming up with Justin. He stepped to the mound and threw a nice easy fastball a little outside and high.

Phil flailed at it and missed.

"That pitch was way out of the strike zone," Luke said. "It wasn't a good pitch to hit. You weren't watching the ball. You were way out in front, and you forgot your level swing."

Brian threw another fastball down and in.

Phil jumped back and sat down hard.

"Stay in there!" Luke yelled. "Pitchers'll try to jam you. You've got to hit that inside pitch."

Phil stepped in again, got his bat back and ready, concentrated as hard as he could. Brian threw a change-up, and Phil belted it into left field.

"Good going!" said Luke. "You always want to hit the top half of the ball. Hit the bottom half and you'll pop up if you don't put it in the seats."

Brian threw some more. Phil hit a few ground balls and a sharp line drive to center. He missed a few, too, but he didn't care. He was getting the rhythm of his swing, getting his timing right, and when Justin came in to relieve, he didn't do so badly with him either.

When the others came to bat, he watched them from the field. Brian crouched really low and had terrific bat speed. Justin lifted his right leg as he strode into the pitch. Jenny and Luke just seemed to be in a groove.

"Okay, bunting. Phil first!" Luke said.

Phil shuddered as Luke got him into the batter's box. "Okay, rule one, same as before. Watch the ball. You were losing it at tryouts. Then arms back, square around and crouch. You weren't crouching either."

Phil tried it. It felt easy.

"One thing. Instead of sliding your right hand up to the bat head, slide both hands up a little. Then bunt the ball off the fat part of the bat. It's easier that way when you have short arms."

Brian threw a few pitches, and Phil laid a few down. No trouble. Just did it. "Now run this one out," Luke said finally.

Phil sort of dawdled down to first.

Luke didn't look happy. "You always run flat out to first. Always!"

Something else he would never forget now. When everyone else had bunted, it was time to go.

"Hey, Phil," Luke said as they walked off together, "want to come to my house for a Coke?"

"Great!" said Phil.

As they left, the old white Chevy behind the outfield fence left, too.

8. It's a Lot of Work, But It's a Lot of Fun, Too

Luke's house was gray on the outside, but it was warm and cozy inside. Everything looked a little worn and frayed. Phil liked being there right away.

He met Luke's little brother, Jamey. He met his mother, who was a nurse. She was tall, with a big deep voice and a friendly smile. They sat around the kitchen drinking their Cokes and talking baseball—Luke's mom was a fan, too—until Luke's dad came in.

He looked exactly like Luke—short and solid—and he was just as nice.

"Hear my boy's giving you a workout."

"Yup," Phil said, "he is."

"It's a lot of work, baseball."

"Yes, but it's a lot of fun, too."

"Hey, that's what I like to hear," said Mr. Emory, and he clapped Phil on the back. Then he invited him to stay for dinner.

Phil called his mom and she said it was okay. They had hamburgers and salad and ice cream and everything was delicious. When he said goodnight to all the Emorys and thanked them before he left for home, he felt terrific.

Then it was Saturday and they worked on baserunning and stealing and sliding and more hitting and fielding practice. Phil came home full of details of his progress, and Sunday morning his dad pulled out his old glove and offered to play catch in the backyard. Phil was so flabbergasted, all he could do was grin. His dad had a good arm, too.

Then it was Monday and school and Brian and Luke, and no guff at all from Pete Wyshansky. It rained Wednesday night and Phil was sure practice would get washed out for Thursday, but the weather cleared and they got in another good workout.

Suddenly, it was Saturday again. Phil got home from the ballfield totally exhausted and happy. He was playing really well. He'd learned a whole lot. His last practice with his new friends might be over, but he knew he'd be playing baseball again. He was good enough to make the team now, even if he hadn't.

He flopped down in his favorite chair and relished the moment. Then his parents walked into the room, both of them together, looking as if something was really wrong.

"Phil?" his dad said.

"Yes, Dad?"

"I feel very bad about this, especially now when things seem to be going so much better for you, but we may have to move again."

"What?"

"I know this is hard. It's hard for us, too, but the job, the new department, may not work out. We won't know for a while, but—"

"Oh, Dad!"

Phil's dad put his arm around him and explained that he wanted the family to be prepared for a move this time, even if nothing ended up happening. They all talked about it some. Then Phil's parents went back to their bedroom.

Phil sat in the living room by himself, watching the shadows on the wall. No miracle would get him on the team now. Even if it did, he wouldn't be around to play. He would lose his friendship with Luke and the others. He would lose everything all over again.

9. Close Call

Sunday morning the phone rang early. Phil knew his parents would still be asleep. He knocked the fuzzies out of his head and ran downstairs to get it.

"Hello, Phil?"

"Yes."

"It's Coach Channing."

"Oh, hi."

"Phil, I have something important to ask you. You know today is our opening game against the Titans."

"Yes."

"Well, I've just learned that Art Weinstock, our third baseman, won't be able to play. He's doing badly at school, and his parents are keeping him out for the season. I realize it's very short notice, but could you possibly join the team at practice before the game? I can't guarantee you'll play, but we don't want the squad to be one short."

The miracle was happening. "Why are you asking *me?*" he blurted.

"I've been watching you work with Luke and the other kids. You've come a long way these last two weeks."

"You were watching me?"

"Remember the Chevy by the outfield fence?"

"But that's not your car."

"My sister's. Look, will you join us?"

"Yes!"

"Good. Meet me at the field at one-thirty and I'll give you your uniform."

He hung up. Phil's head was spinning. All that work, all that time—he wanted to run upstairs and wake his parents!

Then he remembered. He couldn't join the team. He wasn't even sure he'd be here!

He'd given Coach Channing a commitment. He had to talk to Luke.

He reached for the phone. Five long rings. A sleepy voice answered "Hullo?"

"Luke, it's Phil. Coach Channing just called. He wants me on the team."

There was a short pause, then, "Hey man, congratulations! I knew you could do it."

"Yeah, but I couldn't have done it without your help."

"Thanks. But tell me, why did the coach change his mind?"

Phil told him about Art Weinstock and the white Chevy.

"No foolin'! I dropped a few hints about us at team practice, but coming by in the car, watching us play—"

"Yeah," said Phil, "Coach Channing is too much."

"Then why do you sound so lousy?"

There it was, the chance to talk about his feelings. The move, the game.

He couldn't do it. "It's nothing," Phil said. "I guess I still can't believe this has happened. See you at the game?"

"Sure," said Luke, "and Phil?"

"Yes?"

"You're gonna be great!"

Those words that should have meant so much made his stomach clench. Even so, he was at the field at one-thirty on the dot. His parents, who were thrilled he'd been chosen, would come later.

A few kids were already there. Coach Channing walked right up to him, shook his hand, and gave him the uniform.

"Really glad you're here, Phil. Change in the men's room at the center. Then come on back to practice."

He walked across the street carrying the uniform. He walked in the door of the center, and there was that long corridor, the same long corridor he had walked down only two weeks before. He walked straight into the men's room and put on the uniform.

It had white pants and a red shirt with white trim. The number eleven appeared in white on the shirt, with ROCKETS across the back. It fit.

He looked pretty good, if he did say so himself.

10. Closer

Back at practice, he ran into Brian, then Justin and Jenny. They pumped his hand and slapped him on the back. "You see," Brian said. "We *knew!*"

They were all in the middle of their warm-ups when Luke showed up. He was late but not enough to count. The coach gave him a look, but that was all. Luke and Phil exchanged a thumbs-up sign. That was the best, but knowing what he knew, Phil couldn't enjoy it much.

And then they were out in the field. In spite of his uneasiness, Phil tried to feel loose and ready to play. Positions didn't seem completely set, so the coaches had him playing all over the infield. He got down, got in front of the ball, stayed within himself, powered those throws to first on a line. The first baseman hardly had to move from his stretch.

At the plate he was like a well-oiled machine. He stroked a few base hits to left, hit a towering fly to center, only missed one or two pitches. By the time the Rockets sat down so the Titans could practice, he didn't know what to expect.

Then Coach Channing read out the starting lineup.

1. Lucas Emory C
2. Phil Hubbard 3B
3. Andy McClellan P
4. Justin Carr 1B
5. Brian Krause SS
6. Pete Wyshansky RF
7. Jennifer Carr LF
8. Michael Wong CF
9. Vicky Lopez 2B

Starting at third? Batting second behind Luke? Phil and Luke stood for a high-five.

The bleachers were starting to fill up. It was getting close to game time, and the tension was starting to rise. The Titans' starting pitcher was a big black kid named Jake Thornton. Phil watched him warming up and saw he could throw hard, maybe even a curve. He decided not to look for his parents. He'd find them afterwards. By the time they'd gone over the batting signs—hit (touch cap), take (fake bunt), bunt (clap)—and he trotted out to third, he'd gone through a couple of bouts of nerves to mix with his guilt.

Even so, he felt good. Every single part of him was focused on the game now.

Nothing much happened in the top of the first. A little pop-up to Vicky Lopez. A routine grounder he scooped up and pegged over to Justin at first. A strikeout. Andy was throwing his usual brand of smoke, and the Titans weren't hitting it.

Unfortunately Thornton was just as tough, and Luke went down swinging on three pitches. The look he gave Phil as he left the batter's box should have been carved in stone.

Phil stepped in and settled himself. He watched the ball.

The first pitch was on the outside corner for a called strike. The second was up and in for a ball. Another was up and in, and Phil fouled it off. Then he got his pitch. A big slow change out over the plate, and he jumped all over it. The ball screeched toward the hole between short and second, but the shortstop ran, dove, and made an incredible catch. It was nothing but a solid out.

As Phil trotted off the field to the cheers of the crowd, Pete Wyshansky yelled, "Tough luck, buntless wonder!"

"Hey," said Coach Channing, "none of that, Pete. We're a team. Forget that, and you're out of here."

Phil was glad the coach had heard, but anything Wyshansky said made him feel lousy anyway.

It got worse in the third inning. By then

the score was tied 1–1. In the top of the second, the Titans put together a run on two walks and a single, but the Rockets came right back when Justin crushed one over the right field fence.

Now there were two out and a runner on second and Big Jim Jacoby, a Titan slugger, coming to the plate. Andy ran the count to 0 and 2, but then he served one up and Jacoby hit a screaming line drive down the third base line. Phil dove for it, but it went by him into left field for extra bases. The run scored, and when Jenny bobbled the ball in left, Jacoby ended up at third.

Andy got out of the inning without any further damage, but the score was now 2–1. Even though Phil knew he wasn't really to blame, he was kicking himself when he came off the field. He'd been inches away! If only he could have gotten there. It was then he heard the raspberry and saw the little smile and wave from Wyshansky at the other end of the bench.

The noise was low enough so Coach Channing wouldn't hear, but it was loud enough to make Phil mad. He was due up again that inning. He knew he'd make the most of it.

So far the Rockets hadn't been able to hit Thornton at all. Apart from Justin's homer, all they had was a walk to Brian Krause. But Luke got up and singled after Vicky Lopez grounded out. Then it was Phil's turn.

He'd never concentrated so hard in his life. Thornton was big and fast and tough, but Phil hung in and fouled off three pitches. Then he reached out and poked one up the middle. As he sprinted for first base, he saw Luke rounding second. As he steamed into second and held up there, Luke scored the tying run standing up.

Leading off second base, Phil heard the crowd chanting *Rah Rah Rockets* as if for the first time. He hoped against hope he'd be hearing it all season.

The score remained deadlocked until the top of the fifth when Thornton slammed a triple into deep right field. That was all for

Andy, and Josh Rubin came in to take his place. Josh promptly gave up a single to center, scoring Thornton, but the action really picked up in the bottom half of the inning.

Josh helped himself by leading off with a single, Justin walked, and Brian drove them both in with a double to left. That was all, but the Rockets were ahead 4–3!

Top of the sixth, and last, inning. The crowd was going crazy. Josh struck out Jacoby with a blistering sidearm fastball. He walked the next batter, and the guy stole second over Luke's throw. He struck out the catcher, Jim Romano, and everyone went quiet. One more out!

Hank Northrop, the skinny left fielder, stepped to the plate. He swung at the first pitch and slammed it into the hole at third. Phil went deep to his left and snagged the ball. The runner from second was already reaching third. Phil set and threw as hard as he could. It was a long throw, but it beat Northrop by a step.

The game was over. The Rockets had won!

The crowd was on its feet. Cheers and high-fives surrounded Phil when he reached the Rockets' bench. Even Pete Wyshansky couldn't stay out of it.

Coach Channing got them all together so they could shake hands with the Titans at home plate, but afterwards they started up again. A few of the guys tossed their gloves at one another. Andy McClellan and Josh Rubin shared a high-five, and Phil, Justin, and Jenny stood on the sideline, shouting "We won!"

When Phil finally found himself back on the bench, he said, "Hey, Brian, remember that play you made at tryouts, the one deep in the hole? I was thinking of how good it was when I made my last throw."

Brian smiled. "You remembered that?"

"This elephant never forgets," said Luke.

And then, as if he'd been hit in the stomach, Phil couldn't escape his feelings any longer. "You're right, Luke," he said, "I

don't ever forget. There's something I have to tell you all."

In a moment, the whole team was around him, prodding, pushing, wanting to be close enough to hear.

"I should never have joined you today," Phil said. "My father's probably going to be transferred. I'll probably have to move again."

There was silence. Phil looked at the ground, his whole world coming apart. He felt Coach Channing coming toward him, but when he looked up, it was his parents he saw instead.

"We're not moving," said his dad. "My boss called before the game. He's going to give the department another chance."

And everyone was cheering again. Teammates jumped up and down, slapping each other on the back. Luke picked Phil up and carried him around. Everyone shouted "Hooray!" and then Coach Channing spoke the words Phil would never forget:

"Here's to a brand new season, with Phil Hubbard starting at third base."